A witch's

CW00548885

Story written by Adrian Bradbury
Illustrated by Eva Byrne

Titch, the witch, is at the shop.

fresh

soft

crisp

5

A can of frog legs.
A tub of slug dip.

In the bag!

Six bat wings.
A pot of rat spit.

In the bag!

A box of soft cobwebs.
A tin of moths.

In the bag!

A witch's lunch. Yuck!

Retell the story

Take turns retelling the story with your child.